Banger and Mash

by Jenny Dale

Illustrated by Susan Hellard

A Working Partners Book

MACMILLAN CHILDREN'S BOOKS

To Norma, Rachel and Jade – with love and
thanks

Special thanks to Narinder Dhami

First published 2001 by Macmillan Children's Books
a division of Macmillan Publishers Limited
25 Eccleston Place, London SW1W 9NF
Basingstoke and Oxford
www.macmillan.com

Associated companies throughout the world

Created by Working Partners Limited
London W6 0QT

ISBN 0 330 48425 7

1 3 5 7 9 8 6 4 2

A CIP catalogue record for this book is available from
the British Library.

Typeset by SX Composing DTP, Rayleigh, Essex
Printed and bound in Great Britain by Mackays of Chatham plc, Kent

Chapter One

"Banger! Mash! You're very quiet up there. I hope you're not doing anything naughty?"

The two brown-and-white terrier pups looked at each other when they heard their owner's voice.

"No, Linda!" Banger barked. He

dropped Bob's slipper, which he had almost chewed to pieces.

"No, Linda!" woofed Mash. He had been happily chewing the other slipper to shreds.

"I think we'd better go downstairs," Banger yapped. He nudged what was left of Bob's slippers under the bed out of sight.

"It was *your* idea to chew Bob's slippers, Banger," Mash yapped back. "You said it would be a really good game."

"It *is* a good game," Banger woofed, "as long as Bob and Linda don't find out."

Quickly the two puppies trotted out of their owners' bedroom and across the landing. Just as they reached the top of the stairs, the doorbell rang.

"It's Mia!" Banger yelped in delight.

"Hang on, Mia," Mash barked urgently, "we're coming."

The puppies almost fell over each other as they scrambled down the stairs. Mia Smith and her mum had only been living next door for three weeks, but Mia had quickly become great friends with Banger and Mash.

Today Linda and Bob were going to visit Linda's mum, who lived a long way away. Banger and Mash had gone with them last time, but they'd found the car journey *very* boring. They'd whined and yapped so much that this time they were going to spend the whole day with Mia instead. And they were really looking forward to it.

"Be careful, you two," Linda laughed. As she came out of the living room, she almost tripped over the two excited pups.

"Quick, Linda," Banger and Mash barked together. "It's Mia!"

They raced down the hall in front of Linda, and waited impatiently for her to open the door.

Mia was standing outside. Banger and Mash rushed out to greet her.

"Hi, Mia," Linda said cheerfully. "Are you enjoying the school holidays?"

"Yes, thanks." Mia grinned at her. "Especially as it means I've got more time to play with Banger and Mash!"

"Stroke me first, Mia," woofed Banger, who was dancing around her ankles.

"No, *me* first," woofed Mash. He jumped up and pawed at Mia's knees.

Mia smiled and bent down to pick the two pups up. Banger and Mash took it in turns to cover her face with kisses. "I *did* have a bath today, boys," Mia laughed, hugging them both.

"It's really good of you to have the pups for us, Mia," Linda said gratefully. "I know you and your mum must be very busy decorating your bedroom."

"Decorating?" woofed Banger, cocking his head to one side. He looked across at Mash. "Mia and her mum are doing some decorating!"

"Brilliant," Mash barked. He wagged his tail so hard, it looked as if it might fall off. "We can help them, just like we helped Bob and Linda decorate the living room last week."

"Are you *sure* the pups won't be in your way?" Linda asked doubtfully. "They were quite a handful when Bob and I were painting our living room last week."

Mia laughed. "I'm sure they'll be OK," she said.

"Of course we will," Banger yapped indignantly.

"Yes, just wait till you see what we can do with a pot of paint, Mia," Mash yapped proudly. "You won't believe it."

"Linda, are you ready to go?" Bob came out of the kitchen, pulling on his coat. "We've got a long drive ahead of us." He grinned when he saw Mia. "Hi there, Mia. Thanks for looking after these two little terrors!"

"We're not terrors – we're terriers," yapped Mash crossly.

Banger and Mash followed Mia next door, while Bob carried over a bag of toys and their drinking-bowls. Then Mia and the puppies stood on the doorstep to wave goodbye.

"Be good, you two," Linda called, as she and Bob climbed into their car.

"Of course we will," Banger woofed.

After Linda and Bob had driven off, Mia took the puppies inside and closed the door.

There was a lot of banging and thumping going on upstairs in the Smiths' house.

Mia's mum appeared at the top of the stairs, looking very red in the face. "Put the pups in the kitchen, and come and help me, Mia," she called. "I can't move your bed on my own."

"Hello, Mrs Smith," Banger yapped, as Mia took them down

the hall to the kitchen. "Don't worry – we'll help with the decorating."

" Yes, we've had lots of practice," Mash woofed proudly.

But then Mia shut the kitchen door on them and ran upstairs!

The two pups sat down, disappointed.

"Oh, well," Banger sniffed. "I'm

sure Mia and Mrs Smith will come and get us to help them before long. Then we'll show them what to do."

Chapter Two

A few minutes later, Mia and her mum came into the kitchen.

"Oh, is it time for us to help now?" woofed Banger, his tail wagging.

But Mrs Smith just smiled and opened the back door. "Come on, you two," she said. "You can play in the garden while Mia and I get on with the painting. We don't want you getting under our feet."

Banger and Mash looked at each other, puzzled.

"But we want to *help*," Mash woofed.

"Yes, we're *brilliant* at decorating," yapped Banger.

"I don't think they want to go, Mum," Mia said, trying not to laugh.

"They'll be fine outside," Mrs Smith replied. "It's a nice warm day, and there's plenty of shade out there if they get too hot." She beckoned to the pups. "Come on, out you go."

Banger and Mash didn't move.

"Out!" said Mrs Smith firmly,

pointing at the garden.

"No-o-o-o-o-o," both puppies howled dismally. And they sat down on the kitchen floor and refused to budge.

In the end, Mia had to pick them up, one under each arm, and carry them outside.

Mrs Smith followed with bowls of water and the bag of toys. Seeing the pups' miserable faces, she gave them a pat. "Never mind," she said. "We'll take you for a nice walk in the park when we've finished the painting." Then she stared from one to the other. "Goodness," she said to Mia. "They're so alike! How do you tell them apart?"

"That's easy," Mia said. "Banger has bigger patches of brown on his face – oh, and two dots on his nose."

"That's right, Mia," yapped Banger and Mash together. "Well spotted!"

Mia gave them a cuddle, then put them down on the lawn.

"Now be good, you two," she said. Then she and her mum hurried back into the house.

Banger and Mash were disgusted. They slumped down on the grass, their ears droopy and their noses between their paws.

"It's not fair," Banger sniffed crossly.

"Tell you what," Mash yapped, his tail beginning to wag a little. "Let's try to get back into the house. Then we can *show* Mia and her mum just how good we are at decorating."

Banger's ears perked up. "How?" he asked.

Mash bounded over to the flower bed next to the back door.

"We can dig a tunnel into the kitchen." He began to scrabble about, sending dirt flying in all directions. "Come on, Banger!"

Banger hurried to join him, and the two pups began to dig furiously. Soon they'd dug quite a big hole.

"Are we any closer to the house yet, Mash?" Banger panted. He

shook the dirt from his brown-and-white coat.

"Not yet," Mash puffed. "Keep digging."

Suddenly the pups heard the sound of Mia's bedroom window being flung open. They looked up and saw Mrs Smith leaning out. She had a paintbrush in her hand and she was wearing a big shirt streaked with yellow paint.

"Banger! Mash!" Mrs Smith shouted crossly. "Stop digging up my roses."

The two pups crept away from the flower bed with their tails between their legs. They slumped down on the grass again.

"Why is Mrs Smith being so mean?" Banger grumbled.

"I bet Mia would let us help," Mash agreed glumly.

The puppies looked at each other. Then they both threw back their heads and began to howl. "Mi-aaaaa! Mi-aaaaa! *Please* let us come in and help."

This time Mia opened the bedroom window and looked down at them. "Be quiet, boys!" she called. "Mum says you have to stay outside, and that's that."

Gloomily, Banger and Mash gave up. They could see that there was no way they were going to be allowed inside the house.

"I hope Mia and Mrs Smith know what they're doing," Banger woofed.

Mash yawned widely. "I'm a bit

sleepy. I'm going to have a nap
while we're waiting." He curled
up in the shade underneath one
of the trees.

But Banger didn't feel sleepy at
all. He played with his favourite
rubber bone for a while. Then he
began to nose around the lawn.

Soon he picked up a very

interesting smell. Banger knew exactly who it was – Fluffy, the big ginger cat who lived in a house across the road. To their disgust, Banger and Mash had once even seen Fluffy in Linda and Bob's garden. But they'd soon chased her out.

"Grr!" Banger growled softly, deep in his throat. "Don't you *dare* come near Mia's house, Fluffy!"

He followed the smell right to the bottom of the garden. *Maybe Fluffy is hiding down there somewhere*, Banger thought hopefully. If she was, he'd chase her all the way back to her own house.

But suddenly Banger forgot all about the big ginger cat. The large shed at the bottom of the Smiths' garden was standing open. Banger's shiny brown eyes lit up. The pups had wanted to look inside the shed since the Smiths moved in, but the door had always been closed.

"Mash!" Banger barked loudly. "Wake up!"

Mash opened an eye. "Go away, Banger," he growled. "I'm asleep."

"The shed door's open," Banger woofed. "And I'm going in."

"Really?" Mash jumped to his paws, his tail wagging hard. "Brilliant!" He dashed over to his brother.

The two pups raced inside the shed and looked around eagerly. They found old furniture, garden tools and cardboard boxes, as well as *lots* of interesting smells.

"There's loads of things to play with in here," Mash yapped happily. He attacked an empty cardboard box and began to tear it to bits.

But Banger wasn't listening. He was staring up at a shelf high above their heads. "Look, Mash," he woofed.

Mash glanced up at the shelf. All he could see on it were a couple of tins of paint. "Come and help me kill this cardboard box," he barked. "It's much more interesting."

"No, you don't understand," Banger woofed, nipping at his brother's tail. "We can use that

paint up there to decorate the
shed. *Then* Mia and Mrs Smith
will see just how good at painting
we are!"

Chapter Three

Mash cocked his head to one side. "That's a brilliant idea, Banger," he barked. "Except for one thing . . ."

"What?" Banger snapped impatiently.

"How are we going to get the paint down?"

"Oh, that's easy," Banger woofed. "I'll climb up onto that table underneath the shelf, and then I'll be able to reach the paint. Simple!"

"And how are you going to get up onto the table?" Mash asked.

"I'll climb onto the chair that's next to it," Banger replied.

"And how are you going to get up onto the chair?" Mash wanted to know.

"I'll climb up that big pile of flowerpots," Banger yapped. "Just watch me."

The plastic flowerpots were stacked up in a higgledy-piggledy way next to the chair. Banger began to climb up them. But as he crept higher, the pile of pots

began to sway from side to side
rather alarmingly.

"Look out, Banger!" Mash
barked anxiously.

Luckily, Banger managed to
scramble safely onto the chair
before the stack collapsed.
Flowerpots flew everywhere. One
of them landed right on top of
Mash.

"Help!" Mash barked, running around the shed with the pot stuck over him like a snail shell. "Everything's gone dark."

"Stop running about," Banger woofed crossly as he climbed onto the table. "You're distracting me."

Mash managed to shake the flowerpot off at last. "Don't knock anything else over, Banger," he ordered, as his brother began to climb again.

The table was covered with gardening tools and packets of seeds. As Banger heaved himself up onto it, he knocked some of the packets to the floor. One of them was open, and seeds showered around Mash like noisy little raindrops.

"Banger!" Mash yelped crossly, as the seeds stuck to his fur. "Look what you've done." He shook himself hard to get the seeds out of his coat.

"Sorry," Banger woofed. He was standing on the table now. By stretching up on his short hind legs, he could just about reach the shelf with his front paws.

Puffing and panting, Banger scrambled up onto the narrow ledge. "I did it!" he barked triumphantly. "Look at me, Mash!"

"Yes, but what are you going to do *now*?" Mash asked. "How are you going to get the paint down?"

"Leave it to me," Banger barked

importantly. "Stand clear, Mash!"

And he gave the first tin a gentle
nudge with his nose. It moved
slowly forward, teetered on the
edge of the shelf for a moment,
and then fell towards the floor.
But, as it fell, the tin hit the table.
The lid shot off and bright blue
paint flew *everywhere*.

Everything in the shed was

splashed with paint – including Mash.

"*Banger*!" Mash howled, staring down at his coat. "I'm *blue*!"

But Banger was too busy nudging the other tin off the shelf to listen. The second tin flew down. As it hit the floor it exploded. And pale green paint covered the floor – *and* Mash.

"Now I'm blue *and* green!" Mash barked.

Banger looked down at his twin. "Hey!" he barked. "That looks great. Now it's *my* turn." He scrambled down, and . . . SPLAT! Banger launched himself into a blue paint puddle, then he ran over and rolled in the green puddle. Soon he was as blue and

green as his twin.

"Wheeee!" Mash barked
happily, as he skidded along the
floor, spraying paint in all
directions. "Decorating the shed is
fun!"

"Who needs paintbrushes?"
Banger woofed. "We can just use
our tails." He wagged his tail at

his brother, flicking spots of paint everywhere.

"And our paws!" added Mash. He started jumping around. His paws left blue-and-green prints all over the wooden floor. "Mia and her mum will *have* to let us help them now."

The pups were enjoying themselves so much that they didn't hear footsteps coming closer to the shed. Suddenly, the door opened wide.

"*Oh!*" Mia gasped. "Banger and Mash, what have you *done*?"

Chapter Four

Banger and Mash looked around and wagged their blue-and-green tails proudly.

"Hello, Mia!" they woofed together. "We *told* you we were brilliant at decorating."

Mia just stood there with her mouth open. She stared at the two blue-and-green puppies, and the paint-covered shed. She was so shocked, she couldn't say anything.

"Look, Mia really likes it," yapped Banger. He playfully nipped his brother's blue left ear. "She likes it so much she can't think of a thing to say!"

"Yes," Mash agreed. "I knew she would. And maybe Mia's left the back door open," he woofed. "This could be our chance to help with her bedroom too."

Banger wagged his green-spotted tail. "Let's go for it!" he barked.

The two pups charged out of the shed and up the garden towards the back door. To their delight,

Mia *had* left the back door open.

"Come back, you two!" Mia shouted, racing after them. But she couldn't help laughing as she watched two blue-and-green bottoms bouncing up the garden.

"Sorry, Mia, can't stop," Banger panted.

"We've got some decorating to

do," Mash puffed. They hurtled into the house at top speed.

"Stop!" Mia yelled. "Mum will go mad if you get paint all over the house."

But it was too late. Banger and Mash raced through the kitchen and up the stairs, leaving blue-and-green pawprints on the wooden floors, all the way.

They ran into Mia's bedroom. Mrs Smith was standing on a stepladder painting a wall. She was concentrating so hard that she hadn't heard the puppies come up the stairs.

"Don't worry, Mrs Smith," Banger barked. "We're here to help now."

"That's not bad," Mash woofed

approvingly, as he looked at the yellow colour on the walls. "But we can make it even better!"

Mia's mum looked round, then gasped as she saw the green-and-blue pups. She almost fell off the stepladder. "Mia!" she shouted furiously. "What are Banger and Mash doing in here? And *why* are they all green and blue?"

Mia hurried into the room. "They were playing with some paint in the shed," she explained quickly.

"Not playing – *decorating*," Banger pointed out.

"And we don't need brushes either," Mash went on. "Look." And he gave himself a shake. Flecks of green and blue paint splashed over one of the yellow walls.

"Mia, look what they've done," Mrs Smith groaned.

"Yes, we're helping you decorate," Banger barked loudly, and he wagged his tail against another wall. A green-and-blue feather pattern appeared.

"Nice work, Banger," Mash yapped admiringly.

"Quick, Mia, catch them!" said Mrs Smith. She began to climb down the stepladder as fast as she could. But she wasn't looking where she was going. And when she reached the bottom, she put her foot onto the lid of the paint pot. "Oh, no!" she cried. She hopped around trying not to drip

yellow paint on the floor.

"You're not as good at decorating as we are, Mrs Smith!" Mash woofed. He and Banger ran around the room rubbing against the walls. They left a green-and-blue trail behind them.

"Get them out of here, Mia!" Mrs Smith shouted. Red-faced, and standing on one foot, she tried to clean her trainer.

Mia dashed over to the pups. But Banger and Mash had come to help decorate and they were determined to finish the job. Banger scampered in one direction and Mash went off in the other. Mia couldn't catch either of them.

"We *told* you we were great at decorating," Banger barked proudly. He shook himself against a patch of wall and added some more brightly coloured specks.

"This is brilliant fun," Mash woofed happily. He jumped up and leaned on a wall with his two front paws to add a few artistic pawprints.

By now Mrs Smith had taken off

her paint-covered trainer, and was chasing after the puppies too. "Shut the door, Mia," she yelled, "so that the pups are trapped in here."

It wasn't so easy for Banger and Mash to avoid being caught now. A few moments later, Mia managed to pounce on Banger. She held him tight. Her mum grabbed Mash.

"Thank goodness!" Mrs Smith gasped. "Now let's get them out of here."

Mia stared hard at the puppy she was holding. Then she looked at the pup in her mum's arms. "Oh, dear," she said. "They're both so covered in paint, I can't tell which one's Banger and which one's Mash!"

"I'm Banger," woofed Banger, licking Mia's cheek.

"And I'm Mash," barked Mash from Mrs Smith's arms.

"It doesn't matter which one's which," said Mia's mum. She stared gloomily round the room. "Just *look* at the mess they've made."

Chapter Four

"What mess?" Banger and Mash yelped. They were very surprised – and a bit hurt too. After all their hard work, the lower half of the boring yellow room now had a *very* interesting blue-and-green pattern.

"Don't you like it, Mia?"

whimpered Mash, hanging his head.

"We were only trying to help," Banger whined. He buried his face in Mia's sweatshirt.

There was silence for a moment or two while Mia stared around her bedroom walls. Then, suddenly, her face split into a big grin. "But, Mum," she said, "it looks like one of those special paint effects from that TV programme – you know, the one where people decorate each other's rooms. And I *love* it!" she announced.

The puppies pricked up their ears. They both stared at Mia. Had she *really* said she liked it? Their tails gave a little wag.

Mrs Smith looked at the walls again. Finally, she said, "Mmm . . . yes . . . I see what you mean." And now she was smiling too.

The puppies' tails wagged like mad.

"Phew," woofed Banger. He gave Mia's chin a lick.

Mash couldn't reach Mia, so he gave her mum a lick instead.

"Well, I think that's *quite* enough excitement for one day," said Mrs Smith, laughing. "We'd better clean our two little artists up, before Linda and Bob get back."

Suddenly Mia looked worried. "Mum, what if the paint won't come off?" Then she gasped. "And what if it's *poisonous*? It might make Banger and Mash ill!"

Mrs Smith shook her head. "Don't worry, Mia," she said. "If they found it in the shed then it's the paint we used in the spare room. I know it's not poisonous, and it will wash off in water."

"Oh, good," said Mia, relieved.

"The sooner we get these two washed, the sooner we can start to clean up in here, and in the shed. I dread to think what a state it's in. Here, Mia, take this one too," said her mum, handing Mash over. "I'll go and fill the bath."

Banger and Mash looked at each other in disgust.

"Huh!" grumbled Banger. "I'd rather be blue and green than have a bath!"

"Me too," Mash agreed gloomily.

Just then, the doorbell rang. Mrs Smith went down to answer it.

In a few moments, she returned – with Linda and Bob!

Chapter Six

"Oh!" Mia cried. "Hello. You're back early."

Linda and Bob smiled and nodded.

"When we got there, my mum was out," Linda explained. "She must have forgotten we were visiting."

Then their smiles faded as they saw the blue-and-green puppies tucked under Mia's arms.

"Is that Banger and Mash?" Linda gasped.

Bob stared at the pups as if he couldn't believe his eyes.

"Yes, it is," Mia admitted, feeling very embarrassed.

But Banger and Mash weren't embarrassed at all. They were wagging their sticky blue-and-green tails very happily.

"Hello, Linda," Banger barked proudly. "We've been doing some more decorating."

"Hi, Bob," Mash woofed. "What do you think of it? Nice, eh?"

Quickly Mia explained what had happened. Bob and Linda were

very apologetic then, after a minute, they both roared with laughter. "They just love messing about with paint," Linda said, pulling Mash's blue ears affectionately.

"We weren't messing about," Mash replied crossly. "We were *decorating*."

Just then, Banger's tummy rumbled. "And after all that hard work, we're starving," he added.

"We were just about to give the puppies a bath," said Mia.

Banger and Mash both started to wriggle. "Can't you feed us first?" they whined.

"I know that sound," Linda said with a grin. "They're hungry. We'd better feed them first, or they'll wriggle too much for us to bath them properly." She rolled up her sleeves and reached out to take Banger from Mia. Then she frowned, staring hard at the puppy. "Hang on a minute, which one is this? Banger or Mash?"

"It's me, Banger, of course," Banger snuffled indignantly.

"I don't know," Mia admitted anxiously. "I can't tell them apart now."

"Don't worry, Mia," Bob said. He grinned. "I know how to sort them out. Let's all go next door and I'll show you."

Linda winked at Bob. Then she turned to Mia. "I think Bob has a *special* supper in mind for Banger and Mash," she said.

Bob nodded, then led the way next door.

"A special supper!" yapped Banger excitedly.

"Linda and Bob must be really pleased with our decorating," woofed Mash from Mia's arms.

Next door, Mia and her mum followed Linda and Bob into the kitchen.

"I wonder how Linda and Bob will tell Banger and Mash apart when they are still covered in paint?" Mia said.

"I was wondering that too," yapped Mash. "My face is still green!"

"Well, we'll soon find out," said her mum.

Bob and Mrs Smith put plenty

of newspaper down in the
kitchen, then Linda and Mia put
the two sticky pups down on the
floor.

Banger and Mash watched Bob
go to the big white fridge in the
corner and open its creaky door.

"I love that noise!" barked
Mash, his tail wagging madly. It
often meant little treats were on
the way. And sometimes a
delicious supper of leftovers from
Linda and Bob's dinner.

"Me too," woofed Banger.

The two pups leaped around
each other in excitement as Linda
put one red and one blue food
bowl on the worktop.

Bob took two foil-covered dishes
out of the fridge. He peeled off

the foil and emptied each dish
into the food bowls. Banger and
Mash jumped up to see what he
was going to give them.

"Can you see what it is,
Banger?" barked Mash.

"Not yet," woofed Banger. He
nudged Bob's leg with his nose
and left a smudge of green
paint.

"Hey, Banger *or* Mash," said Bob with a grin. "Don't cover *me* in paint too."

"I'm Banger, and I just want to know what we are having for supper," yapped Banger.

"It's ready now, boys," said Bob, putting the food bowls on the kitchen floor. "Eat up quickly before all that paint dries, or we'll never get it off."

Mia was very surprised to see that the blue bowl was filled with bits of cold sausage, and the red bowl was filled with mashed potato.

"Yippee!" Banger barked happily, rushing towards the blue bowl. "Sausages – my favourite."

"Hurray!" Mash woofed, charging over to the red bowl. "Mashed potato – *my* favourite!"

The hungry pups buried their noses in the bowls, and started eating happily.

Mia began to laugh. "So *that's* why they're called Banger and Mash!" she exclaimed. "We

wondered why they had such funny names, didn't we, Mum?"

Mrs Smith nodded. She was laughing too.

"Of course, they don't get sausages and potatoes *every* day," Bob said with a grin. "But luckily, we had some left over from last night – which is just as well. They'll need their favourite treat before being scrubbed in the bath."

Mash looked up from his bowl. "Of course we do," he barked. "We worked really hard decorating Mia's bedroom."

"That's right," yapped Banger. "It isn't easy when you have to use your tail *and* paws."

"I hope they didn't cause too much trouble," Linda said to Mia and her mum. "Bob and I will come over later and help you clean up."

Then she turned to Mia. "Are you sure you like your walls with green and blue splashes?" she asked doubtfully.

"Oh, yes," Mia said firmly. "And once the new carpet's down, it will look great. We won't be able to see the pups' pawprints on the floor – or Mum's trainer-marks either!"

"In fact I might even decorate my bedroom tomorrow in the same colours," Mrs Smith added.

Banger stopped eating, and pricked up his ears. "Did you

hear that, Mash?" he barked.
"We're decorating Mrs Smith's
room next."

"Oh, brilliant," Mash woofed.
"Eat up all your sausages, Banger
– we're going to be working hard
again tomorrow!"